Hi! I'm Darcy J. Doyle, Daring Detective, but you can call me D.J. The only thing I like better than reading a good mystery is solving one. When I found a map in an old book I bought at the Bayside Public Library book sale, I thought it would lead to a box full of missing money. What it led to was a whole bunch of trouble! Let me tell you about The Case of the Troublesome Treasure.

Books in the Darcy J. Doyle, Daring Detective Series

Darcy J. Doyle
Daring Detective

The Case of the
Troublesome
Treasure

Linda Lee Maifair

ZondervanPublishingHouse
Grand Rapids, Michigan

A Division of HarperCollins*Publishers*

The Case of the Troublesome Treasure
Copyright © 1996 by Linda Lee Maifair

Requests for information should be addressed to:

📖 ZondervanPublishingHouse
Grand Rapids, Michigan 49530

Library of Congress Cataloging-in-Publication Data

Maifair, Linda Lee.
 The case of the troublesome treasure / Linda Lee Maifair.
   p. cm. — (Darcy J. Doyle, daring detective ; #9)
 Summary: Hoping to find a buried treasure by following clues left in
an old library book, D.J. and her best friend finally discover what is really
valuable.
  ISBN: 0-310-20734-7
  [1. Buried treasure—Fiction. 2. Friendship—Fiction. 3. Mystery
and detective stories.] I. Title. II. Series: Maifair, Linda Lee. Darcy J.
Doyle, daring detective ; #9.
PZ7.M2776Cax 1996
[Fic]—dc20   96-15112
                                                                   CIP
                                                                    AC

Edited by Lori J. Walburg
Interior design by Rachel Hostetter
Illustrations by Tim Davis

Printed in the United States of America

---

96 97 98 99 00 01 02 03 /❖ DC/ 10 9 8 7 6 5 4 3 2 1

*To my "writing angel" Margery Facklam,
who helped me believe in Darcy—and myself.*

CHAPTER 1

I'm Darcy J. Doyle. Some of my friends call me Darcy. Some just call me D.J. If I keep solving important cases, pretty soon everyone will be calling me Darcy J. Doyle, Daring Detective. It's only a matter of time.

My last big case started when I went over to where Nick Rinaldi and Sammy Lee were rummaging through a big stack of books at the Bayside Public Library used book sale.

Nick pulled a book with a worn blue cover from the bottom of the pile. "Wow! Look at this!" he said, holding it up for me to see. "A really old collection of Sherlock Holmes stories!" He gave me a sly grin. "You've heard of Sherlock Holmes, haven't you?"

Nick was the only client who had ever fired me—right in the middle of *The Case of the Giggling Ghost*. He never let me forget it. He and Sammy Lee were always making jokes about my detective work. And just about everybody at Bayside Elementary knew that Sherlock Holmes was my all-time favorite detective.

I ignored his question. "Are you going to buy it?" I said. I nodded toward the book, trying not to show how much I wanted it myself.

Nick looked at the price sticker on the back. "Only fifty cents," he said. He leafed through the pages with Sammy Lee peering over his shoulder.

"Pretty good condition, for such an old book," Sammy Lee said.

Nick nodded. "Except for here ..." Sammy Lee pointed out a place on the inside of the back cover. "... where the paper needs to be glued down a little."

I held my breath while Nick inspected the cover and thought it over. He grinned at me again and

8

handed the book to the lady behind the book counter. "I'll take it," he told her.

I held my breath again when he started searching his shirt and jeans pockets for the money to pay for it. He made a sour face. "I, uh ... don't seem to have the money," he told the lady. He turned to Sammy Lee. "Can you loan me fifty cents?"

Sammy Lee shook his head. He held up a stack of paperbacks. "I spent all my money on riddle and puzzle books."

The book-counter lady set the book back down on the table. "Then I'm afraid you can't have the book, young man," she told Nick.

I picked it up.

"That will be fifty cents." The book lady held out her hand.

"I, uh, don't have the money either," I told her. I had saved up eight dollars for the book sale, but I'd spent it all on mystery books.

I turned to the book lady. "Could you hold the book for me?" I asked. "For just a few minutes?"

She nodded. "I suppose so. But if somebody else comes along with the money to pay for it, I'll have to let him have it."

Nick's wide, challenging grin set me running off in one direction while he and Sammy Lee ran off in the other. I found my best friend Mandy sitting on the floor in the corner reading one of the horse books she'd bought. "I ... need to ... borrow ... fifty cents," I told her breathlessly.

She looked up from her story. "Sorry, D.J.," she said. "All I have left is a quarter." She reached into her fanny pack and pulled it out. "But you can have it if you need it."

I glanced over to Nick Rinaldi, who was talking to a couple of other boys from school. "Thanks!" I grabbed the quarter Mandy held out to me, then took off at a run again.

Usually I never go out of my way to find my pesty younger brother, but this was an emergency. I knew just where to look. He was at the snack table, stuffing himself as usual. "H ... h ... hi,

Allen!" I panted. "I'm glad . . . to see . . . you!" I put my arm around his shoulder.

He held a half-eaten brownie far away from me. "Why?" he asked suspiciously.

It took a promise to take his turn doing dishes and a reminder that I'd spent half the weekend helping him with a social studies project to get him to loan me the quarter. I even had to sign an IOU.

I scribbled *I owe Allen Doyle 25 cents* on his chocolate-smeared napkin, signed my name, stuffed the napkin in his hand, took the quarter, and ran. I beat Nick Rinaldi, who had a dollar in his hand, back to the book table by about two seconds. "Here!" I said to the book lady, holding out two quarters stuck together with chocolate icing. She made a face as I plopped them into her palm.

I wiped my hands on my jeans before adding Sherlock Holmes to the pile of books in my shopping bag. When I looked up, Nick was still standing there holding his dollar. "I hope you're not too disappointed," I told him. "You can borrow it to read sometime if you want to."

"That's OK," he said. "You need it a lot more than I do."

"Yeah." Sammy Lee grinned at me. "So you can learn how a *real* detective works!"

If I hadn't liked the book so much, I might have thrown it at them!

CHAPTER 2

Max was waiting in the yard for me when I got home. He ran up and stuck his head in my shopping bag.

"He loves mystery books too," I told Mandy.

"Yeah, right," she said. "Almost as much as he likes those cheese crackers I gave you."

I pulled Max's head out of the bag and stuck my hand inside, fishing around among the books until I found what was left of the pack of cheese and peanut-butter crackers Mandy had shared with me. "Do you mind if I give them to Max?" I asked her.

Mandy wrinkled her nose at the two squashed crackers oozing peanut butter out the side of the package. "Be my guest," she said.

I never saw cheese crackers disappear so quickly. When Max was done licking the peanut butter off the roof of his mouth, he and Mandy and I went up to my bedroom to put my new books away. I squeezed them all onto the bookshelf Dad had made for me. All except Sherlock Holmes.

I took a bottle of glue out of my desk drawer, plopped down on the bed, and opened the book to where the paper had come loose.

"That's funny," I said.

Mandy came over and stood beside me. "What's funny?"

"I thought the glue had just dried out or something, but this looks like it was cut." I showed her the straight, smooth slit in the paper on the back binding. "Like somebody did it on purpose."

"Why would somebody do that?" Mandy asked.

I ran my fingers across the paper. "There's something under here," I told her. "Something lumpy between the paper and the hardcover."

I went back to the desk and got my scissors. Then I carefully slid one blade under the paper to lift it up and away from the hardcover backing. "It's a folded sheet of paper," I said, peering inside the opening I'd made.

I used the tip of the scissors blade to catch the corner of the paper and pull it out. Even though it was folded, I could see that there was writing on the inside. "It's a note or something," I said.

Mandy was as curious as I was. "Who'd stick a note inside a book cover?" she asked.

I didn't know, but my Daring Detective mind was anxious to find out. I carefully unfolded the paper. "It looks like a map," I said. "Of Bayside." I pointed out the crude drawings of the courthouse, the Bayside High School building, and the old railroad station that had been turned into a fancy restaurant.

"Look at this!" I told Mandy. There was a date in the upper right-hand corner of the paper. *November 18, 1947.* "That's . . . that's . . ."

Mandy was better at math than I was. "That's almost fifty years ago!" she said. She pointed to the five lines of crooked printing at the bottom of the map. "What do you suppose all that means, D.J.?"

I read the list.

1. Tower of Justice. North. Golden triangles.
2. Main door. Third steeple.
3. Hero's tomb. 3482 steps east.
4. Inside gate. 39th picket left.
5. Bank box. Three feet down.

I read the last line again. Twice. "If it means what I think it means, Darcy J. Doyle, Daring Detective, is going to be rich, Mandy!"

"I don't get it," Mandy said.

"Think about what it says," I told her. "*Bank box. Three feet down.* Some robber hid his loot somewhere in Bayside, and I'm going to find it! I bought more than a book today, Mandy. I bought myself a map to a buried treasure!"

Mandy's mouth dropped open. But before she could say anything, Allen came stomping into the room, waving the smudgy napkin with my IOU. "I want my quarter back, Darcy," he said. "You said you'd pay me as soon as we got home."

"Not now," Mandy told him. "Darcy was just explaining to me about our treasure."

"*Our* treasure?" I asked.

She nodded. "You would never have bought the book ... or found the treasure map ... if I hadn't loaned you that quarter."

Allen is only smart about two things. Food and money. "There was a treasure map in the book we bought?" he asked Mandy.

"*We?*" I said.

He nodded the same way Mandy had done. And his eyes had the same strange gleam. "If she gets part of the treasure, then I should get part of the treasure," he said. "I loaned you a quarter too, you know!" He waved the chocolaty IOU under my nose to prove it.

Like any good investigator, Max wanted to get a closer look at the evidence. He grabbed the napkin and took off with it, barreling down the stairs with Allen, Mandy, and me screeching close behind.

CHAPTER 3

A man down at the newspaper office showed us how to work the microfilm machine.

"Here we go," he said, squinting at the screen. "November 1947. A very popular month and year. Had somebody in here looking at the same film just last week. Just turn this crank to move it forward or backward till you find what you're looking for."

"Thanks," I told him. "We appreciate all your help."

"No problem," he said. "Like I told the other kid, I think it's really commendable that somebody your age would spend your Saturday afternoon doing research in some dusty old newspaper basement. Must be something your class is doing for school, huh?" he asked.

"No, sir. Just a little project I—" Mandy poked me in the ribs from behind. Allen kicked the back of my right shoe. I corrected myself. "—*we're* working on." Pointing out to Allen and Mandy that the map was in *my* book so it was *my* map, and all I really owed them was a quarter, each, hadn't done much good.

"*Together*," said Mandy, who had threatened not to speak to me ever again if I didn't share the treasure with her.

"*Partners*," said Allen. Unfortunately, he hadn't threatened not to talk to me. But since I'd given in and let Mandy in on the treasure, I knew it wouldn't be very fair to try to keep Allen out of it.

My "partners" gathered in close on either side of me, looking at the screen over my shoulder as I cranked through the microfilmed newspapers from November 1947. Pages whizzed by before I found what we needed. "Here it is! The eighteenth!" I said.

"Look at that headline!" Mandy screeched into my left ear.

"The map must be for real!" Allen squealed in my right.

I put a hand over each ear and read the headline. *Search Continues for Bayside Bank Robbers*. The article below the headline told how the state and county police were looking for two men who had robbed the Bayside Bank of more than $60,000.

The article on November 16—*Bayside Bank Hit by Armed Bandits*—told about the robbery itself.

And the article on November 22—*Robbers Found: Money Missing*—explained how the thieves had been captured, but the money had not been found.

"Sixty thousand dollars!" Allen whispered.

The math was even easy enough for me to do in my head. "That's twenty thousand dollars each!"

Right away we thought of a zillion ways to spend it.

"Computer games," said Mandy. "And clothes. And riding lessons at Baymount Stables!"

"Amusement park passes," said Allen. "And video games. And in-line skates and pads and helmet."

"A whole wall of bookshelves filled with mystery books!" I said. "And a trip to Disneyworld."

"Anything we want!" said Mandy.

"Everything we want!" said Allen.

"*If* we can find the treasure," I reminded them.

Mandy clapped me on the back. "It'll be easy with Darcy J. Doyle, Daring Detective, as our partner. You've probably figured out where the money is already."

I took out the map and read the clues again. "Well, at least I know where to start," I told Mandy. "The courthouse!" I looked at the clock on the wall above the microfilm machine. Four o'clock. "And I have only an hour to get there before it closes!"

"*We*," Mandy corrected.

"*Partners*," Allen reminded.

"Only because I'm so generous," I told them. "The whole sixty thousand dollars should really be mine. All I really owe either one of you is a quarter."

We argued about it all the way home to get Allen's Cub Scout compass and all the way back downtown to the courthouse. Three very grumpy looking partners huffed and puffed up the winding stairway to the observation deck on the old clock tower.

"How do you know this is the right place to start?" Allen asked.

I read the first clue aloud. *"Tower of Justice.* This is the courthouse, isn't it? Where criminals are brought to justice. And . . ." I motioned to the walls around us. ". . . this is a tower."

"What was the rest of it?" Mandy asked. "North . . ."

"North. Golden triangles," I read. "Which way is north, Allen?"

The way Allen squinted at his compass, I could see how his whole Cub Scout den had gotten lost—twice—on their last orienteering hike. "Over there," he finally decided. He pointed to the observation window to our left.

We raced to the window and stared through the finger-smeared glass at what we could see of Bayside.

"There!" Allen yelled, pointing to two large, gold-yellow shapes a few blocks away. "Golden triangles."

I shook my head. "Those are golden arches, not triangles, Allen. And I'm pretty sure that McDonald's wasn't here in 1947." I stared out the window again. "I don't see ..."

"There!" Mandy said. She pointed to the top of Wilton's Department Store. A whole row of gold painted brick triangles decorated the top of the building, all the way around, just below the roof. "Lots of golden triangles. And Wilton's has been around *forever!*"

"Let's go!" Allen started pulling me toward the stairway.

Mandy looked like she was going to cry. "I can't," she said. "I have to be home by five-thirty. We're going to my grandmother's for dinner tonight."

"Allen and I don't have to be home until six," I said. "We can go and check it out and—"

"No way, Darcy Doyle!" Mandy interrupted.

I was surprised at how mad she looked. "Huh?"

"You and your brother aren't going off and finding that treasure without me," she told me.

Now *I* was mad too. I was her best friend, and I didn't like what she was hinting. "Why?" I demanded. "Do you think we'd cheat you or something?"

Mandy folded her arms across her chest. "I think maybe you should let *me* keep the map until tomorrow," she said.

"No way, Mandy Thompson!" I crossed my arms over my chest too.

If the courthouse security guard hadn't come up and told us the tower was closed, we might have stood there glaring at each other all night.

CHAPTER 4

Pastor Jordan's sermon the next morning was about greed and jealousy. For some reason, it made me uncomfortable. I squirmed in my seat and kept glancing over in Mandy's direction all the way through it.

"I hope Mandy Thompson was listening!" I whispered to Allen when we stood for the closing hymn and prayer.

"Yeah," Allen whispered back. "Me too."

We were supposed to meet Mandy at her house at two o'clock. But Mom got a glimpse of Allen's room and made him clean it up before he could go anywhere. And of course, he wouldn't let me go on without him.

"It's not that I don't trust you," he said, looking like he didn't trust me one little bit. "You know how it is."

"Yeah, I know," I said. I was beginning to see just how it was. First with my best friend. Now with my brother. I didn't much like what the chance to get some of the treasure—some of *my* treasure—was doing to them.

It took Allen almost an hour to find his bed and get all his clothes and toys off the floor. We didn't get to Mandy's house until almost three o'clock. Mandy wasn't there.

"She's gone to get the treasure without us!" Allen squealed.

We ran all the way to Wilton's. Mandy was sitting on the steps in front of the main entrance. She did not look happy.

"You were supposed to wait for us!" I told her.

Max went over to dig in a big flowerpot next to Mandy.

"And you were supposed to be there at two o'clock," she said.

Max stuck his head in a trash can behind Allen.

"You went after the treasure without us!" Allen complained.

Mandy didn't deny it. She stood up and put her hands on her hips. "How was I to know you didn't do the same thing?"

Max took great interest in a fire hydrant over at the curb.

I put my hands on my hips too. "Good thing *I* kept the map," I said. "Otherwise ..." I stopped. There we were, two best friends, glaring at each other. It made the grilled-cheese sandwich I'd eaten for lunch do a flip-flop in my stomach.

A car went by with a barking German shepherd leaning out the window.

Max pulled me to the corner, barking back all the way.

"Good old Max," I said, planting my two feet firmly on the sidewalk and dragging him to a stop. I was grateful for an excuse to stop the argument. "He wants us to get on with the case," I told Mandy.

"*You're* the one with the map," she reminded me.

I couldn't believe she was being so stubborn! Especially when *I* was being so reasonable. I gave her one of my looks before I took the map out of my pocket. *"Main door. Third steeple,"* I read. I would be glad when we found the treasure and she started acting like a best friend again.

"Well, this is the main door," Allen said. He stared up at Wilton's Department Store. "But I don't see any steeples."

"They don't put steeples on stores, Allen," I told him. "They put them on churches."

We looked up Chesapeake Avenue. "No steeples there, either," Allen said.

We looked down Chesapeake Avenue. "Down there!" Mandy said, pointing to a tall, gray wooden spire with a white wooden cross on top. "There's St. Michael's steeple."

"That must be the first one," I said. "Come on."

We had to go halfway down the next block before we found the second steeple. At the Bayside Church of Christ. "That's two!" Allen said.

Number three was Grace United Methodist. "This must be it!" Mandy said. "What's next, D.J.?"

I hated to admit it, but it felt sort of good to have her calling me D.J. again, even if it did sort of slip out by accident. I read the next clue on the map. *"Hero's tomb. 3482 steps east."*

"Where would we find a hero's tomb?" Allen wanted to know.

That clue wasn't too hard for my daring detective mind to figure out. I pointed to the fenced-in yard at the side of the church. "Probably in a graveyard," I said.

I tied Max's leash to the post of the NO PETS ALLOWED sign outside the cemetery gate and led the way inside.

"Let's split up and look around," I told Allen and Mandy.

They both eyed me suspiciously. Neither one budged.

"Oh, all right!" I snapped. "We'll look around together!"

The three of us went up and down the rows of tombstones. Me in the front, and Mandy so close behind me she kept stepping on the back of my sneakers. As for Allen—he was so close I could smell on his breath the onions and horseradish he had put on his grilled-cheese sandwich. When we found a grave with a star and a flag on it, we thought we'd found what we were looking for. JOHN P. CARPENTER. BORN 1932. KILLED IN ACTION 1951.

"He was a hero, wasn't he, Darcy?" Allen asked me.

I nodded. "But he's not the one we're looking for. This tombstone wasn't around when the robbers made the map."

"WOOF! WOOF! WOOF, WOOF, WOOF!"

I looked up to see what Max was barking at just as a pizza delivery car pulled up to the curb across from the church.

"Is food all that dog ever thinks about?" Mandy asked.

I gave her another one of my looks. "Food nothing!" I told Mandy. "Good old Max is telling me where to find the hero's tomb!"

"Where?" Mandy asked. "Down at Dominic's Pizza Parlor?"

"No," I said. "Right over there!" I pointed across the graveyard to the statue of a large, shaggy dog. "Remember the story Miss Woodson told our class about Molly, the dog who rescued the kids from the fire at the Bayside Orphanage a long time ago?"

"Yeah!" Mandy said. "The dog kept running back into the burning building to bring the children out. When she died, the city council paid for a statue for her grave site because she was such a—"

"*Hero!*" Mandy, Allen, and I said at the same time.

Max was still barking. Even though he was facing the parked pizza car instead of the graveyard, I smiled smugly. "See," I told Mandy. "My faithful bloodhound Max knew it was a dog hero we should have been looking for all along."

"Yeah, right," Mandy said.

CHAPTER 5

We counted out 3,482 steps, exactly, east of Molly's tomb.

It wasn't easy. There were buildings and trees and a couple of backyard swimming pools along the way.

The trees weren't too much of a problem, except when there were birds or squirrels in them Max wanted to chase. But we had to guess how many steps it would take to walk straight through the buildings, since we couldn't do it. And when Max saw a bunch of kids playing volleyball in one of the swimming pools, the temptation was too much for him. He jumped right in.

I managed to let go of his leash in time, but Mandy couldn't get out of his way. He knocked her right in with him. Max thought it was a great game. He chased her a couple of laps around the pool before he let her get out again.

"You made him do that—on purpose!" Mandy said. She stood at the edge of the pool wiping water from her arms and legs and face with a clean towel somebody had given her.

I tried not to laugh, but it wasn't easy. "I did not!" I told her. "Why would I?"

She used the towel to wring out her hair. "So I'd have to go home," she said. "To change clothes. So you'd have the chance to go and get the treasure without me. Just like you've been trying to do ever since we found the map!"

I was tired of being accused of trying to cheat her. "I'm the one who found the map," I reminded her. "And it looks like I'm the one who should be worried. After all, you're the one who pushed your way into this, loaning me a quarter and expecting me to pay back twenty thousand dollars of *my*

money instead! You'd probably take the whole thing if I gave you the chance."

"I'm not going home to change until we find the money!" Mandy said.

"If you want to walk around town dripping wet, that's up to you," I told her.

"And after we get the treasure and split it up, I never want to speak to you again, Darcy Doyle!"

I tried to tell myself I didn't care. And I wasn't about to let her know it mattered to me one way or the other. "Why wait until then?" I said. "You can stop speaking to me right now!"

She did. In fact, none of us said a word until we got to where the rest of the 3,482 steps had been leading us.

"Uh-oh," Allen said then.

The fifth clue said, "*Inside gate. 39th picket left.*"

We'd found the gate. And the 39th picket inside to the left.

"Uh-oh," Mandy agreed, talking to Allen, not to me.

The 3,482 steps had brought us back into our own neighborhood. Right to the backyard of Miss Winifred Merriweather. President of the Bayside Garden Club, who had come to our science class a few weeks ago and spent a whole hour talking about aphids and beetles.

The gate was part of a spotless white picket fence all the way around Miss Merriweather's garden.

The 39th picket to the left of the gate was right in back of one of Miss Merriweather's prize rosebushes. The one in the newspaper photo Miss Woodson had tacked to her bulletin board at school.

"Uh-oh," I said myself.

The three of us stood there wondering what to do.

"We could wait until dark," Allen suggested. "Then we could sneak in and—"

"Allen Doyle, you have video games and in-line skates and amusement park tickets on the brain," I scolded. "Digging up her garden in the dark wouldn't be any better than digging it up in broad daylight."

Mandy sighed in frustration. "The treasure couldn't be in a worse place if somebody planned it," she said.

Even though she was still talking to Allen and not to me, something in what she'd said made my daring detective stomach feel all queasy. I decided it would be a long time before I could look grilled cheese in the face again.

A window went up on the side of Miss Merriweather's house. The smell of fresh-baked apple pie wafted out as she set a pie on the windowsill to cool. A big, barking ball of reddish-brown fur leaped into the air and took off toward the window, drooling all the way.

Good old Max. He's never one to sit around when there's a case to be solved. I took off after him. "MAAAAAXXX! STOOOOPP!" I yelled.

CHAPTER 6

Chasing aphids and beetles must give you really good reflexes. Miss Merriweather peeked out the window and snatched the pie from the ledge about two seconds before Max would have grabbed it.

Max was running so hard, he slid nose first, up to the shoulders, right through the open window. Allen, Mandy, and I plowed into each other not far behind.

"What's going on here?" Miss Merriweather demanded. She was holding the pie up high over her head, out of Max's reach.

"My faithful bloodhound Max was anxious to interrogate you," I told her.

"I beg your pardon?" she said.

I tried again. "I'm Darcy J. Doyle, Daring Detective. This is my faithful bloodhound, Max." I got a grip on Max's collar and pulled him down away from the window, Miss Merriweather, and her pie. "And these ..." I nodded toward Mandy and Allen. "... are my, uh ... partners." I wasn't very happy about it, but it sounded better than *pesty brother* and *ex-best friend*. "We're on a big case, and we need to ask you a very important question."

"And what question is that, dear?" Miss Merriweather wanted to know. She looked very much like she was trying not to smile.

"Well, uh ... You see we, uh ..."

My youngest partner blurted it out. "We want to know if we can borrow a couple of shovels and dig up your rose garden," he said.

Miss Merriweather didn't slam the window. And she didn't throw the pie at us or call the police. She did laugh, though. For a long time. "Why on earth would you want to do that?" she asked.

"It's kind of a long story," I warned her.

She smiled. "I've got lots of time. Why don't you and your partners come in and have a piece of warm apple pie and ice cream and tell me all about it."

She didn't have to ask twice. In fact, my reddish-brown, furry partner went in through the window. The rest of us used the front door.

I told Miss Merriweather about finding the map in the book. About going to the newspaper and reading about the robbery. About following the clues to the courthouse, Wilton's Department Store, the Grace cemetery, and right to her backyard.

"Aren't you clever," she said. "And isn't it nice that you all work so well together."

Mandy and Allen and I stared at the red checkered tablecloth on Miss Merriweather's kitchen table. We hadn't been working very well together at all.

Miss Merriweather looked from me to Allen to Mandy. "You're lucky to have friends you can count on," she said. "Good friends are hard to find."

I was beginning to feel like an aphid or beetle. I was really glad when Miss Merriweather changed the subject. "May I see the map?" she asked.

I took it out of my pocket and gave it to her. She studied it for a few seconds. Then she shook her head. "I'm afraid you should have been looking for the mapmaker instead of the money," she told us.

I handed Max the last bite of my pie crust and let him lick the apple-cinnamon juice from my fingers. My queasy feeling was back, and I knew it wasn't from the pie I'd just eaten. "What?" I asked Miss Merriweather.

She gave me the map. "I'm afraid this is a hoax. You know, some kind of practical joke," she said.

Allen actually stopped eating. Right in the middle of a heaping forkful of his second piece of pie. "You mean there's no treasure?"

"I doubt it very much," Miss Merriweather told him. "For one thing, the Bayside High School pictured on the map wasn't built until 1950. I was a junior there the year it opened. And I had the picket fence put in when I bought the house ten years ago. To keep the neighborhood kids from taking shortcuts through my garden. It wasn't here in 1947 either."

I took out my notebook and pencil.

"What are you doing, D.J.?" Mandy asked, letting the nickname slip out again.

"I've spent two days following a bunch of phony clues somebody left for me," I said. "Now I'm going to make a list of the real clues and see if I can figure out who it is."

"Can I help?" she asked.

I didn't remind her that she never wanted to speak to me again. I'd already lost a treasure. I didn't want to lose my best friend too. "You're my partner on this case, aren't you?" I told her.

I looked over at Allen, slumped in his chair, pouting over his pie plate, thinking about the video games and in-line skates and amusement park tickets he wouldn't be able to buy now. "And that goes for you too, Allen Doyle!" I said. He looked up and managed a small grin. Even if he was a pest, it was good to see him smile.

I started making a list of all the things we knew about the map and the mapmaker, writing each clue down beside the name of the person who thought of it, D for Darcy, M for Mandy, A for Allen:

A: *Found the map in the book.*

D: *Bought the book at the book sale.*

M:*Nick Rinaldi found the book first.*

D: *Nick knew I liked Sherlock Holmes.*

A: *The man at the newspaper office said some kid had been there doing research on November 1947.*

M:*Nick heard the story about the hero dog Molly in class with the rest of us.*

D: *Nick was there when Miss Merriweather came to class. He saw the picture on the bulletin board.*

A: *Nick and his friends like to play practical jokes.*

It didn't take much to figure out who the culprit was. I was just surprised at how many clues there had been—and annoyed at myself for not seeing them sooner. Nick Rinaldi had made up the map and put it in the book. Then he'd pretended to find it at the book sale, knowing how much I'd want the book and that I'd find the map inside.

"Why would he play such a trick on you?" Miss Merriweather asked.

I told her about *The Case of the Giggling Ghost*. "He's always making jokes about what a terrible detective I am. How I'm always jumping to conclusions and following the wrong clues. Calling me things like Darcy Doyle, the Detoured Detective."

I tossed the phony treasure map on the table in front of me. "I guess he was right all along," I said.

"No, he wasn't, D.J.!" Mandy protested. It was good to have her sticking up for me again. "You're a really good detective!"

"Yeah," Allen agreed. "Sooner or later you always figure it out, even if it does take you a while."

Miss Merriweather gave me a sly, daring detective sort of smile. "Maybe it's time your friend Nicholas found that out for himself," she said.

CHAPTER 7

Mandy and I walked into Miss Woodson's classroom on Monday morning carrying a stack of catalogs.

Electronics catalogs. Video and computer catalogs. Toy catalogs. Sporting goods catalogs. Clothes catalogs. Tour catalogs for cruises to the Bahamas, train tours of Canada and Alaska, and plane trips to neat places like Ireland. We'd gone door-to-door in the neighborhood and collected a great big pile of them.

We carried them right past Nick Rinaldi and plopped them down on top of my desk two seats behind his. Nick didn't say anything, but he did look curious. Especially when Josh Henderson said, "What are you two up to, D.J.? Taking up weight lifting?"

I laughed. "No. Spending money."

Nick was part of the crowd that gathered around my desk.

"Lots of money," Mandy added.

"A whole bag of money!" I said.

"Where'd you get a whole bag of money?" Sammy Lee wanted to know.

"Found it. Under a prize rosebush," I told him.

Nick Rinaldi's eyebrows went up in surprise, which didn't surprise me one bit.

"Oh, sure," Sammy Lee said. "My mother always hides money under her rosebushes. Makes them grow better."

"Nobody put the money there to make the roses grow, Sammy," I told him. "A couple of robbers hid the money there a long time ago."

Mandy smiled broadly. "And we found it. Yesterday."

Nick was just about to open his mouth to say something when Miss Woodson came into the room and made Mandy and me put all the catalogs away until recess.

Nick Rinaldi kept looking over his shoulder at me all morning. When recess finally came, he was one of the kids who stayed inside to look over our shoulders at the catalogs instead of going out to the playground.

"I found three new games I want for our home computer," Mandy said.

She read the descriptions out of her catalog while the kids around her "oohed" and "ahhed."

"I'm going to get these mountain bikes for my whole family. With one of these fancy side carts for Max to ride in," I told her.

Cheryl Klein's eyes widened in surprise. "Those bikes are *eight hundred dollars apiece!*" she gasped.

"Yeah, I know," I said. "And the cart is six hundred, but good old Max is worth every penny."

"I'm taking my family on this train trip to Alaska," Mandy said. She read about the trip, and the kids "oohed" and "ahhed" again.

It was too much for Nick Rinaldi. "You're not going to Alaska," he told her.

Mandy gave him an innocent smile. "What?"

"And you're not buying any dumb old cart to haul your dog around in, Darcy Doyle!"

"Why, Nick," I said. "Whatever do you mean?"

"You know very well what I mean," he said. "You're making the whole thing up. You didn't find any money under any roses."

I resisted the urge to say, "*Ah ha!*" I had figured out who the culprit was and had almost cornered him into making a full confession. "And just how would you know that, Nick Rinaldi?" I demanded.

"Because," he said, "nobody would be dumb enough to believe a story like that."

It wasn't exactly the full confession I'd been expecting. I pulled a piece of folded paper out of my pocket. "I found this map in that old Sherlock

Holmes book I bought on Saturday morning." I waved it under Nick's nose.

"So?" he said.

"So I did what any good detective does. I followed the clues and they led right to you, Nick Rinaldi. That's how you knew there was no treasure. It was just another one of your practical jokes. You drew the map."

"I did not," Nick said. He looked me right in the eye and didn't blink or twitch or wriggle or smile when he said it.

"You *didn't?*" I said, showing a lot more surprise than I'd wanted to. I had been so sure. It wouldn't have been the first time Nick Rinaldi had tried to pull this kind of joke on me. And all the clues had fit together so well.

I tried to ignore the chuckles and stares all around me as I ran through everything again in my head, starting with Nick finding the book at the Bayside Library book sale. Then one particular chuckle got my attention, and all the pieces fell into place.

"No, *of course* you didn't!" I told Nick, trying to sound as if I'd known it all along. I whirled around to face the person who had pointed out the tear in the binding of the book to be sure I wouldn't miss it. The person who loved riddles and puzzles. "Because *he* did!" I pointed my finger at Sammy Lee's nose.

Sammy Lee's face turned red. "When did you figure it out?" he asked me.

I didn't exactly answer the question. "Any good detective could have figured it out right away," I told him. I was about to tell him all a good detective had to do was look up the date Bayside High was built. Or notice that the map was drawn with a marker pen, which wouldn't have been around in 1947.

Sammy Lee shook his head disgustedly. "It was the copyright date on the Sherlock Holmes book, wasn't it?" he said. "I should have known that was too obvious."

I nodded. "Way too obvious," I agreed. I reminded myself to check it out as soon as I got home.

November 18, 1947

1. Tower of Justice, North, Golden Triangles.
2. Main Door, Third steeple
3. Hero's tomb. 3482 steps east.
4. Inside gate. 39th pickett left.
5. Bank box, Three feet down.

"I guess you're a better detective than I thought," Sammy Lee admitted.

Mandy's a good friend. She didn't tell him anything different. "I can't believe we weren't even speaking to each other, D.J.," she said later, at lunch. "All because of a silly piece of paper."

She apologized, and so did I.

She sighed. "Still, just a *little* treasure would have been nice."

I remembered what Miss Merriweather had said. I broke the chocolate bar Mom had packed in my lunch into two pieces. Then I handed half to Mandy, even though it was my absolute favorite kind. "Anybody can find a treasure," I told her, "but good friends are hard to find."

Mandy thought I would throw away Sammy Lee's phony treasure map, but I didn't. I took it home and put it in my scrapbook of important cases solved by Darcy J. Doyle, Daring Detective, where it would remind me that the real treasures God gives us are worth far more than money.

Collect them all . . .

Mystery and adventure combined with Christian values make great reading for kids ages 7 to 10, and the Darcy J. Doyle, Daring Detective series have just that. Both boys and girls will enjoy piecing together clues and solving mysteries with Darcy J. Doyle, the Daring Detective, along with her faithful "bloodhound," Max, in this funny, fast-paced, and easy-to-read series.

The series contains 12 volumes and can be read in any order. Both avid and reluctant readers will enjoy following the adventures of the not-too-perfect Darcy, the always helpful Max, and the pesky younger brother, Allen. Purchase them individually or purchase them all at once!

 The Case of the Mixed-Up Monster

ISBN 0-310-57921-X

 The Case of the Giggling Ghost

ISBN 0-310-57911-2

 The Case of the Choosey Cheater

ISBN 0-310-57901-5

 The Case of the Pampered Poodle

ISBN 0-310-57891-4

The Case of the Creepy Campout

ISBN 0-310-43271-5

The Case of the Troublesome Treasure

ISBN 0-310-20734-7

The Case of the Bashful Bully

ISBN 0-310-43291-2

The Case of the Sweet-Toothed Shoplifter

ISBN 0-310-20735-5

The Case of the Angry Actress

ISBN 0-310-43301-0

The Case of the Bashed-Up Bicycle

ISBN 0-310-43305-3

The Case of the Missing Max

ISBN 0-310-43311-8

The Case of the Nearsighted Neighbor

ISBN 0-310-20737-1

ZondervanPublishingHouse
Grand Rapids, Michigan

A Division of HarperCollins*Publishers*